Be Truthful

Dear Parent:

Don't be disheartened if your young child tries to cover up his or her wrongdoings or mistakes. And don't be alarmed by frequent and less-than-accurate protestations of innocence. Since being truthful is not a particularly meaningful idea for the very young, such behavior is to be expected. It's more important for young children to feel secure about their parents' love. Before developing a viable conscience, children are intent on avoiding getting caught doing things that grown-ups say are wrong. In fact, not getting caught is of much greater concern than doing the right thing.

Of course, despite all this, we want to guide children toward being truthful. And at the same time, we want them to follow directions and obey our rules. Children come into this world with the simple wish to have all their urges gratified, but only gradually will their quest for parental approval begin to temper those most basic desires. In fact, it will take even more time and maturity for a child to comply with the dictum to "Always tell the truth, no matter what the consequences." In *The Magic Ball*, Clifford confronts this end-game expectation.

You'll notice, however, that Emily Elizabeth does not withhold love or lose faith in her big red dog when he covers up his own error. Instead she seizes the opportunity to explain how important it is that she and Clifford are able to count on each other. Sure, accidents may happen, she allows, but most things that go wrong can be made right as long as we know we can trust each other at all times.

Adele M. Brodkin, Ph.D.

Visit Clifford at scholastic.com/clifford

ISBN 0-439-22467-5

Library of Congress Cataloging-in-Publication Data is available

10 9 8 7 6 5 4 3 2 1   01 02 03 04 05 06

Printed in the U.S.A.   24
First printing, December 2001

Clifford THE BIG RED DOG®

The Magic Ball

Adapted by Peggy Kahn

Illustrated by Carolyn Bracken
and Ken Edwards

**Based on the Scholastic book series
"Clifford The Big Red Dog"
by Norman Bridwell**

From the television script "Special Delivery"
by Larry Swerdlove

SCHOLASTIC INC.
New York   Toronto   London   Auckland   Sydney   Mexico City
New Delhi   Hong Kong

Are you the sort of person
People know that they can trust?
When you have a job to do,
Do you tell yourself, "I must"?

Clifford is my big red dog.

I count on him—

That's true!

He'll do important things

As well as I, myself, might do.

But has it ever happened,
Even with your best intention,
That things start going very wrong—
Things you neglect to mention?

If an accident has happened,

Have you tried to hide the mess?

Or are you always wise enough

To speak up and confess?

One day I gave Clifford

An important job to do.

Listen to this story.

Has this ever happened to you?

Cousin Laura's birthday was coming.

Her present was wrapped with care.

I sent Clifford off to mail it

In time to get it there.

Maybe he met his dog friends
While he was on his way.

Maybe Cleo grabbed it.
Cleo *loves* to play!

"What's in the package,
Clifford?
Let me give it a shake!"

"It's Cousin Laura's present.
Be careful!
It might break!"

"Emily wants it in the mail.
It has to go today.
Give it to me, Cleo—
This isn't a time to play!"

"Say! What is this funny thing?

A pizza?

It tastes yucky!"

"It might be a Magic Ball!

Now wouldn't that be lucky?"

Maybe T-Bone pressed the place
That fills the ball with air.
I can't tell for certain
Because I wasn't there.

I'm sure somehow that beach ball

Was blown up and inflated.

Clifford and his dog friends

Were probably fascinated.

Knowing Clifford, as I do,

I'll bet my shoes and socks

He tried to fit that big, round ball

Back in the small, flat box.

"Oh, no! Clifford!"

"Stop!"

POP! POP!! POP!!!

The mailman said he saw Clifford:

"Your dog was in a trance."

Did Clifford imagine Magic Balls

Doing a magical dance?

Clifford crawled into his doghouse.

I'm sure he was sad as could be.

Do you know what makes Clifford happy?

He's happy when he's pleasing me!

I think his dog friends convinced him

To pretend that all was well.

"Don't show Emily the ruined ball."

"In other words—
Don't tell!"

So . . .

Clifford pretended that all was well.

I brought him a yummy treat.

That so embarrassed Clifford,

He moaned and could not eat.

Then I saw Laura's present—
Broken and deflated.
I understood why Clifford
Was oh, so aggravated.

"Clifford, this is terrible.
Why did you hide the toy?
You should have told me right away.
Don't *ever* fib, big boy."

Luckily, we still had time
To buy another gift.

We hurried to the toy store.

Clifford gave me a lift.

We rushed to the post office.
Now the present is on its way
Straight to Cousin Laura—
In time for her special day!

I count on my dog, Clifford,

And Clifford can count on me

To understand accidents happen

And appreciate… honesty.

BOOKS IN THIS SERIES:

Welcome to Birdwell Island: Everyone on Birdwell Island thinks that Clifford is just too big! But when there's an emergency, Clifford The Big Red Dog teaches everyone to have respect—even for those who are different.

A Puppy to Love: Emily Elizabeth's birthday wish comes true: She gets a puppy to love! And with her love and kindness, Clifford The Small Red Puppy becomes Clifford The Big Red Dog!

The Big Sleep Over: Clifford has to spend his first night without Emily Elizabeth. When he has trouble falling asleep, his Birdwell Island friends work together to make sure that he—and everyone else—gets a good night's sleep.

No Dogs Allowed: No dogs in Birdwell Island Park? That's what Mr. Bleakman says—before he realizes that sharing the park with dogs is much more fun.

An Itchy Day: Clifford has an itchy patch! He's afraid to go to the vet, so he tries to hide his scratching from Emily Elizabeth. But Clifford soon realizes that it's better to be truthful and trust the person he loves most— Emily Elizabeth.

The Doggy Detectives: Oh, no! Emily Elizabeth is accused of stealing Jetta's gold medal—and then her shiny mirror! But her dear Clifford never doubts her innocence and, with his fellow doggy detectives, finds the real thief.

Follow the Leader: While playing follow-the-leader with Clifford and T-Bone, Cleo learns that playing fair is the best way to play!

The Big Red Mess: Clifford tries to stay clean for the Dog of the Year contest, but he ends up becoming a big red mess! However, when Clifford helps the judge reach the shore safely, he finds that he doesn't need to stay clean to be the Dog of the Year.

The Big Surprise: Poor Clifford. It's his birthday, but none of his friends will play with him. Maybe it's because they're all busy. . . planning his surprise party!

The Wild Ice Cream Machine: Charley and Emily Elizabeth decide to work the ice cream machine themselves. Things go smoothly. . . until the lever gets stuck and they find themselves knee-deep in ice cream!

Dogs and Cats: Can dogs and cats be friends? Clifford, T-Bone, and Cleo don't think so. But they have a change of heart after they help two lost kittens find their mother.

The Magic Ball: Emily Elizabeth trusts Clifford to deliver a package to the post office, but he opens it and breaks the gift inside. Clifford tries to hide his blunder, but Emily Elizabeth appreciates honesty and understands that accidents happen.